The Beastie Book

Written by Penny Harter

Illustrated by Alexandra Miller

At night when I am fast asleep
Strange beasties find my dreams.
Some are scary, some are nice,
And some are in-between.

The Beasties

Apple-Clop

The Apple-Clop's a happy beast
Who lives out by the sea
And always has an apple feast
Prepared for you and me.

He buries apples in the sand,
He throws them in the air.
He tosses them to wiggle-fish
Who come to see him there.

If you should go to visit him
It's best to go at night.
You'll find him rolling on the beach
Beneath the bright moonlight.

He'll let you climb the silver dunes
To share an apple pie
And play with him until the sun
Comes bouncing up the sky.

Brahkey

When you meet a Brahkey,
She'll offer you some tea
And ask you for a bedtime tale
Beneath the Bumble tree.

And if you tell a good one,
She'll whinny with delight
And ask you please to tuck her in
With stories every night.

rackle

Beware of the Crackle—
She's under that log.
She knows how to juggle.
She hides in the fog.

Her long arms are stirring
The dead leaves and dirt
As she searches for beetles—
A crackling dessert.

She'll reach out to grab you
And gnaw on your shoe.
And if you aren't careful
She'll juggle with you.

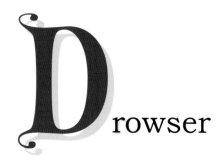Drowser

The Drowser always wakes at dawn
When birds begin to sing.
The sunrise makes her yawn and yawn
Upon her leafy swing.

She opens up her mouth so wide—
Anything can fall inside!

Every-Lap

The Every-Lap is very old.
He lives where it is really cold
With all the snowballs he can hold.

You'll find him in a snow cave there
Where he lives without a care.
You can join him if you dare.

He likes to fill his lap with snow
And toss his snowballs to and fro
Whenever icy storm winds blow.

His frosty fur is quite a sight,
And if you visit him some night
He'll want to have a snowball fight.

loatkin

The Floatkin likes soap bubble rides,
That's how he goes to school.
That's how he gets from here to there
Across the thorny cruel.

Sometimes he wants some company
As he goes floating by,
So he'll invite you to jump in
His bubble in the sky.

He'll take you to his special cloud—
A place he likes to play,
And then he'll take you home again
Until another day.

Gallop-Galore

Come jump on the back of the Gallop-Galore.

He's swift as the wind on a wuthering moor.

He'll take you to somewhere you've not been before

Where everything's quiet except for his roar.

You'll climb up the bump-knots, you'll nibble on slab,

You'll gallop through mountains where Whinnies go mad,

And when he slows down to a crawl like a crab

He'll slide you off gently and call you a cab.

oop-Loon

It's hard to see the Hoop-Loon
Way out on the river.
She always sings at twilight
And her singing makes you shiver.

She sounds extremely lonely
When you hear her mournful tune.
But really she's quite happy
Calling to the moon.

She drifts on quiet waters
And you hear her from afar.
She swims in gleaming circles
And dips her beak in stars.

Iffenproof

The Iffenproof lives on the moon
Because she loves to jump
She bounces off the moony hills
And comes down with a thump.

Sometimes she sits inside her cave,
Counts down from ten to one,
Does long division with the stars
And multiplies the sun.

And when she finishes her work
She whistles at the sky,
And all her answers whistle too
As they go shining by.

Jestilia

You'll find the Jestilia eating a fish
On the banks of a faraway stream.
She washes her toes and she washes her dish
In water that looks like whipped cream.

For dessert she likes strawberry shortcake and jam
Which she covers with dollops of water.
Then she swims to her bed in an old beaver dam
And sings lullabies to her daughter.

 eep-Cross

You shouldn't hug a Keep-Cross
Or scratch behind his ears.
You shouldn't share your toys with him
Or cry him any tears,

Because he's sometimes nasty,
Because he sometimes growls,
Because he seldom smiles at you,
Because he often scowls.

But if you want to try it,
If you want to dare,
If you think he's lonely
And you truly care,

Then go ahead and hug him,
Go ahead and try,
Go ahead and smile at him
And maybe he'll reply,

"I'm not really nasty,
I'm not really bad.
I thought you didn't like me much
And that's what made me mad."

Lopsy-Tilt

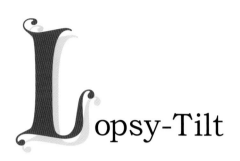

The Lopsy-Tilt can't ride a bike—
He wobbles till he falls.
He cannot even fly a kite
Or learn to throw a ball.

Poor thing, he's better upside down—
He's happier that way.
And if you visit Lopsy-town
He'll pester you to stay.

So you will be all Lopsy too,
And Lopsy-play with him,
And grow a lot of Lopsy fur
Upon your Lopsy skin.

Mackram

Watch out for the Mackram—she's coming today.

She's trying to find you and make you obey.

Her horns have been tossing her horrible hay,

And her eyes are so scary they'll turn you to clay.

So run far away if you hear her loud bray.

The Mackram is coming. Get out of her way!

Ninny-Yap

Yap, yap the Ninny-Yap
Hates to take a Ninny-nap.

He yaps in the morning,
Yaps all night,
Yaps to the left
And yaps to the right.

He yaps at you,
He yaps at me—
He even yaps across the sea.

And so he never goes to sleep
Till he collapses in a heap.

opsy

The Oopsy ties her shoes wrong
And never combs her hair.
Sometimes she doesn't brush her teeth
Or clean her messy lair.

Her shirts are buttoned crooked,
Her socks don't match at all,
And if you try to help her out
She'll only start to bawl.

Perambulo

The Perambulo is funny.
He lives among the trees.
He's always in a hurry
Because he has to sneeze.

He likes to visit spiders
And dig into the dirt,
And if you come upon him
He'll try to climb your shirt.

He'll use it for a tissue
To blow his shiny nose
Unless you say "God Bless You!"
And offer him a rose.

Queriello

You can hear a Queriello
From very far away—
All he does is whine and whine
Every single day.

His voice is like a foghorn,
His face a sorry mess.
He smears his tears and runny nose
And never stops to rest.

He whines about his breakfast,
Complains about his lunch,
Says he doesn't like his food
Because it doesn't crunch.

He isn't very happy,
So all he does is cry.
He runs around a sorry swamp—
Let's make him a mud pie.

Rumplus

If you ever have a picnic
Out upon your lawn,
Watch out for the Rumplus
Who eats the whole day long.

He loves the taste of hotdogs,
Smears catsup on his fur.
He'll eat up all the salads
And steal your hamburger.

He'll drag away your chicken
And take your ice-cream cone,
Or throw a boiled egg at you
Before he goes back home.

You'll never see him coming
Until he's almost there—
Best make a plate to give him
And let him have his share.

piny-Scrowl

When you stumble on a briar patch
In the middle of the night,
You can be sure a Spiny-Scrowl
Has planted it in spite.

Her sharp beak is for digging
Deep holes for little seeds
Of nasty tasting vegetables
She plants among the weeds.

Her babies growl with hunger
For the prickly plants she grows.
She brings them some each morning
Stuck in her spiny toes.

Tumble

What's that in the distance
Tumbling down the hill
With a round yellow body
And a bright yellow bill?

It's a Tumble on her way
To a party by the lake,
And if you want to follow her
You'd better bring a cake.

Her bill looks like a duckling's,
Her tummy's like a moon,
She really wants to dance with you
And quack a happy tune.

So go on, find the party
And have a lovely time
Dancing with the Tumble
Until it's time to dine.

Umfillumpticus

The Umfillumpticus can fly
Above the summer trees.
She spreads her sunlit scarlet wings
And drifts upon the breeze.

She's very scared of lightning
And thunder makes her jumpy.
She doesn't even like the rain
Because it makes her grumpy.

So when a sudden thunderstorm
With lightning rumbles by,
She tries to get back to her nest
And cover both her eyes.

If you should find her in a tree,
Hiding from the thunder,
Get your umbrella from the porch
And please invite her under.

Vocalyptus

Can you hear the Vocalyptus?
His voice is very loud.
He wants to be on TV shows,
perform before a crowd.

He thinks his voice is perfect,
His songs the best there are.
Too bad he doesn't sing in tune—
He'll never be a star.

But all the birds adore him
Because he tries so hard,
And so he loves to sing for them—
That's him out in your yard.

hoofus

The Whoofus lives in a hollow log.
His fur is long and grimy.
He likes to chew on lollipops
And roll in dirt and swampy spots
Until he's really slimy.

He wants to find a family
Who'll love him as their own,
But first he needs a bubble bath
And to find the forest path
That leads him to your home.

Xylock

The Xylock nests on mountaintops
Where she can be alone.
She's always been extremely shy
And hates the telephone.

She never talks to others there.
No one has heard her sing.
She blinks her eyes for yes and no
But will not say a thing.

If someone really cared enough
To climb up to her nest,
She might decide to come on down
And play with all the rest.

Yaballoo

You will not see the Yaballoo
Unless you sail the sea.
She hasn't lived inside a zoo
Or underneath a tree.

The Yaballoo turns somersaults
Among the foaming waves.
She dives into the ocean deeps
And lives in coral caves.

Though she's as big as any shark
She's really very sweet.
She only feasts on seaweed stew
And never nibbles feet.

Sometimes she takes a little nap
Upon a sandy shore,
And then swims out to sea again
To somersault some more.

eedunk

What the Zeedunk likes to do
Is run and run and run.
He runs between the jungle trees
And leaps in pools of sun.

His fur is soft and milky white,
His eyes are brightest blue
And sparkle in the darkest night
As he laps up shining dew.

He often races with the moon
In its trip across the sky,
Tries to touch the silver stars
That gleam as he goes by.

Tonight when you are fast asleep
He'll run into your dream
And take you for a moonlit ride
Beside a starry stream.

For Bill

"A Zeedunk and a Brahley went to sea..."

And for Nancy Flaherty, Charles Bihler, and Courtney and Conor Flaherty,
my wonderful children and grandchildren
Penny

For my awesome daughters, Ronnie & Krissy --
Dream big and work hard.
All my love,
Alexandra

Inquiries should be addressed to Shenanigan Books, 84 River Road, Summit, New Jersey 07901

Library of Congress Cataloging-in-Publication Data

Harter, Penny.
 The beastie book : an alphabestiary / written by Penny Harter ; illustrated by Alexandra Miller.
    p. cm.
 ISBN 978-1-934860-05-2
1. English language--Alphabet--Juvenile poetry. 2. Alphabet--Juvenile poetry. 3. Animals--Juvenile poetry. 4. Bestiaries--Juvenile poetry. I. Miller, Alexandra, ill. II. Title.
 PS3558.A6848B43 2009
 811'.54--dc22   2009031283

Printed in China 1 first edition October 2009
This product conforms to CPSIA 2008